For Freddie and Matilda, with love
~ M. C. B.

For Coral Bahrani
~ T. M.

Copyright © 2012 by Good Books, Intercourse, PA 17534
International Standard Book Number: 978-1-56148-768-4

Text copyright © M. Christina Butler 2012
Illustrations copyright © Tina Macnaughton 2012
Original edition published in English by Little Tiger Press,
London, England, 2012
LTP/1800/0384/0412 • Printed in China

Library of Congress Cataloging-in-Publication Data is available.

One Starry Night

M. Christina Butler   Tina Macnaughton

Good Books

Intercourse, PA 17534, 800/762-7171, www.GoodBooks.com

One clear, bright night, Little Hedgehog
saw a shower of shooting stars sparkle and
flash across the sky.

"Wow!" he gasped. "I must tell everyone!"
And off he ran.

"Have you seen the shooting stars?"
Little Hedgehog called out, as Fox
and Mouse walked home through
the meadow.

"I've seen three!"
cried Rabbit, hopping up
and down.

"Can we stay up to watch them—please?"
squeaked the baby mice.

"All right," said Mouse. "And let's get Badger,
so we can all see them together."

They rushed into the woods, but a huge
tree had fallen across the path.

"We can't get over that!" Little
Hedgehog cried.

"I can," said Rabbit, scrambling onto
the tree. "Give me a hand, Fox."

So Fox pushed
and Rabbit pulled
until everyone was
over on the other side.

Puffing and giggling, they arrived at Badger's house.

"What's all this?" he said.

"Shooting stars, Badger!" cried Little Hedgehog. "Come and see!"

"There are hundreds and hundreds!"
squeaked the mice.

"Wonderful!" said Badger. "Let's go to
the top of the hill. We'll see them better
from there."

As they marched on, the babies began
to sing: "*Twinkle, twinkle, little star!*"

"*How we wonder what you are!*" joined
in Badger.

"*Shining brightly, flashing by,
Like a sparkler in the sky!*" laughed Fox.

"I'm going to catch a shooting star!"
Rabbit called out, racing ahead.
Higher and higher he
jumped when suddenly . . .

he fell down an old badger den! "Rabbit!" yelled Little Hedgehog, and they all raced to help.

But as they peered into the
hole, the sides crumbled and
everyone tumbled in . . .
BUMPETY, BUMP! CRASH!

"Is everyone all right?" coughed Badger.

"Fine," replied Rabbit. "Except Fox is squashing me!"

"And we're stuck down a hole!" snapped Fox.

"We're going to miss the stars!" sniffed one baby mouse.

"We'll find a way out," Badger said. "Don't worry."

Rabbit and Mouse sang
songs with the babies
as the others looked
for a way out.

"I've found another tunnel!"
Little Hedgehog cried.

They climbed out into
the fresh, night air and
ran to the top of
the hill at last.

High above, the sky glittered
with shooting stars.
    "We made it!" laughed
Little Hedgehog. "What a night!"
    And together the friends gazed
happily at the sparkly sky which
stretched on and on forever . . .